This Ladybird Book belongs to:

_____

_____

_____

_____

D0034527

This Ladybird retelling
by
Joan Stimson

Ladybird books are widely available, but in case of
difficulty may be ordered by post or telephone from:

Ladybird Books – Cash Sales Department
Littlegate Road Paignton Devon TQ3 3BE
Telephone 0803 554761

A catalogue record for this book is available
from the British Library

Published by Ladybird Books Ltd Loughborough Leicestershire UK
Ladybird Books Inc Auburn Maine 04210 USA

FAVOURITE TALES

The Sly Fox
and the
Little Red Hen

illustrated
by
BRIAN PRICE THOMAS

based on a traditional folk tale

Once upon a time, there was a little red hen who lived all by herself in a little house in the woods.

She kept her little house neat and tidy, and she did all her own washing and cooking and cleaning. Every day she went out with her little basket to pick up sticks for her fire.

Near the little red hen there lived a sly young fox. He lived with his mother in a den underground.

Now the sly young fox had one big ambition. He wanted to catch the little red hen and eat her! He kept making plans to trap her, but the little red hen was too clever for him, and she always got away.

One day the sly young fox thought up a very cunning plan indeed.

"Put some water on the fire to boil," he told his mother. "Tonight we shall eat the little red hen for our dinner."

With that, the sly fox picked up his bag and crept through the wood to where the little red hen lived.

The sly young fox hid behind a tree and waited.

Before long, the little red hen came outside and began to collect sticks for her fire.

She didn't notice the sly young fox, and she didn't shut her door. The minute her back was turned, the sly fox slipped quietly into her house.

When she was ready, the little red hen carried her sticks inside. As soon as she shut the door, she came face to face with the sly young fox!

The little red hen was terrified. She dropped her basket and flew up to a high beam, right under the roof. The fox could not reach her there, so she felt safe.

The little red hen looked down from her high perch. "You can't catch me now, Mr Fox," she cried. "You had better go home, because I won't come down!"

"We'll soon see about *that*," said the sly young fox with a grin. And he began to run round in a circle, chasing his tail.

Round and round went the sly young fox. Then round and round again, faster and faster.

The little red hen looked down from her perch and watched the sly fox. Soon she felt her head going round and round too!

She became so dizzy that she fell...

…straight into the sly young fox's bag!

"Who said I couldn't catch you?" cried the fox. And, slinging the bag over his shoulder, he set off for home.

Inside the sack, the little red hen kept very still, hoping for a chance to escape.

Before long the sly young fox sat down to rest. After a while he began to doze.

As soon as the fox was asleep, the little red hen popped her head out of the bag and crept away.

Quickly she collected some large stones and put them into the bag. Then she ran all the way home.

When the sly young fox woke up, he
had no idea what had happened.
He picked up his bag and set off
for his den.

"This bag feels really heavy," he said
to himself. "The little red hen must be
fatter than I thought. What a tasty
dinner she'll make!"

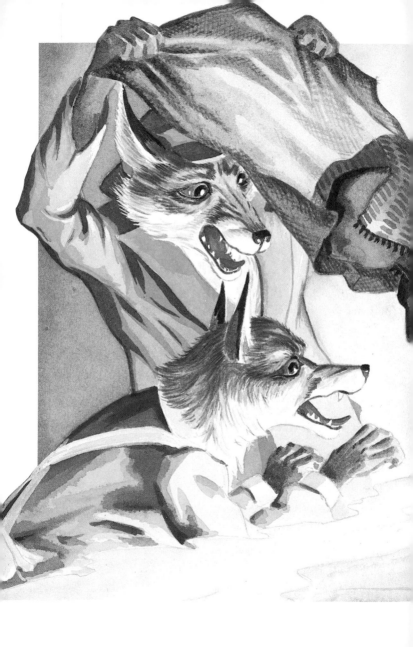

As soon as he reached his den, the sly young fox shouted to his mother, "I've got the little red hen at last! I do hope the water is boiling."

"It certainly is," replied his mother.

So the sly young fox opened the bag over the boiling pot. The stones fell... *SPLASH!*... right into the water.

The boiling water splashed all over the two foxes and killed them both.

By this time, of course, the little red hen was back in her little house in the woods.

There she lived, safe and contented, for the rest of her days.